The Sea

Madeline Konrad

Pink Hydra Press

2025

Copyright

The Sea
© Madeline Konrad 2025

Cover artwork © Stella LaRoh

For Stella, my little star.

i.

I DON'T REMEMBER HER FACE.

That isn't surprising. Time has really gotten away from me. Not that I haven't kept dutiful watch over the passage of the stars, their eternal dance. Even from in here, yes.

Look at me. Talking like a sage. Well, give it a few years, I'll have my silver yet.

What do I remember?

I remember she was always careful with her words. Nothing was wasted. I always struggled with this. Words flow through me like the stars through the Monastery looking-glass. For her, a carefully-placed word would topple an entire edifice of mine.

But there I go, mixing my metaphors again. This isn't working.

I always hated those writers, by the way, who said, *hold on, I should start at the beginning*. I think I have more empathy for them, now.

Well, here goes.

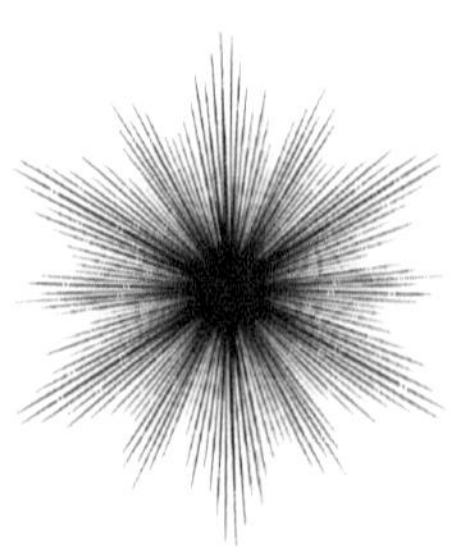

I DO REMEMBER THE OLD STORY.

You know the one. The Queen, last of her line, in the frozen reaches of the East. The betrayal. I saw the players perform it once, before I even started the long, broken road for my silver.

No, I wasn't serious before. How would I earn it now?

I remember the flash of the blade, the handmaiden's strike. Act five, scene three.

I saw it every night, back then. At the beginning.

But, in the way of dreams, the Queen wore my brother's face. And his face I remember even now. Memory is a torment to me, never a balm.

Every night.

I was on the path of silver, as I said. I had my place in the monastery, a full Sister. Little wonder, then, that I would find myself seeking the solace of the stars, when sleep fled from the nightmares of my mind.

Solace. But not, alas, solitude.

" 's your move, princeling."

I hated when Dusty called me that. He knew it, too. I didn't bother even rolling my eyes at him, just slid the white stone home as I kept my face where it was *supposed* to be—fixed upon the stars above.

I did give in a little, muttering, "Seventeen moves, Dusty. You're slipping." Just loud enough for him to hear.

Dusty made a choking sound, but I had not lied. His Queen was pinned, and by one as lowly as a spear-carrier. A piece so unimportant it was rarely ever carved into a distinctive shape.

The choking resolved into an irreverent laugh as Dusty conceded, placing his Queen's piece on its side. "So I am, Sister Elegy. So I am."

I think he was young enough yet that he hadn't procured the first of his many canes—and yet, in my mind's eye, I cannot see him without his left hand grasping for it, planting it firmly on the stone of the Observatorium as he rose to his feet.

I do know that he never used my name—my *proper* name—unless he had good reason to. Over the years, he invented nearly a dozen names for me, *princeling* only the first—and the kindest. I was "Sister Elegy" that night only because I'd won.

But he was always a gracious loser. That, I respected. And it was hard not to love him, after all that time. It's harder, now.

"You've time for another?" he asked as he smoothed over the place where once—he had assured me—he'd sported a proper beard. I had my doubts.

"No. The Starlit Mother is to relieve me in about an hour's time, and I don't think I can beat you again in fewer than twenty moves. I'll give you time to retreat before she arrives."

Dusty snorted. "The Mother herself? Are you sure?" He just wanted another game in, but had no other reason to disbelieve me.

I nodded, and for the first time since he set up the board that night, turned to look him in the eye. He wilted a little, but rallied and said, "Well, I'll see you at the rising, I suppose. Princeling."

And with a wink, he lumbered to the stairs and was gone.

I turned back to the sky. When I had first arrived here, I'd sweat through my nights of vigil, keeping fastidious notes as quickly as the stars and planets rose. Long experience had turned the sacred night into an old friend, each major star and celestial event duly recorded in shorthand with half a thought from me, and barely a glance at the chronometer at my side. Even now, if I close my eyes, I can still see the night sky entire.

The night was, after all, almost predictable.

Almost.

A flash of purest starlight jolted me from my vigil. I dropped my pen and scrabbled for it as I mentally noted the time.

Precisely midnight.

I noted down the flash and time on paper, then looked up to the sky again. And drew in a slow, rattling breath.

The flash had been a star, I realized. One that had fallen from its place.

And it hung in the air, steadily growing brighter—closer.

A distant fear jolted through my heart. But my hand remained steady, even as—

Another flash, and the sound of thunder.

A warm breeze swept across my face, trying its best to undo my bun. It was no more successful than my brother had been, when he lived.

I blinked away the afterimage, the darkness of the night slow in returning. My left hand gripped the side of my wooden seat. I relaxed as a realized I was in no immediate danger.

Below the Observatorium, in the wide, rocky field of grass atop the monastery mount, I saw a figure move. A dim, clear light illuminated the figure, and it took a long moment for me to connect two points in my mind.

When I did, I stared in disbelief.

The figure paused upon a rock, and though the distance was too far for me to tell, I imagine I saw them raise their head to the high stone monastery. They could have seen me atop the Observatorium tower, just as I saw them.

They waved.

The incongruity of that gesture shocked me from my icy posture. I hurried down the outer stairs of the monastery, grateful that it was high summer and the ice that normally haunted those stone steps had long melted.

It feels like the space of a single breath separated those two moments, but the distance would have made that impossible. Regardless, soon enough I stood upon the grassy field, and I could see the . . . well, the visitor . . . closer.

Hair of silver-white hung over a brown, shining face. I noted the combination as something I'd never seen in any lineage on Melodia, even among the throngs of humanity that every hour converged upon the Capitol.

I said I did not remember her face. But I do remember the hue of her eyes—how could I not? They were as dark as the cosmos, with starlight gleaming deep within.

I admit, my long stare taking the whole of the visitor

in—they were perhaps a span shorter than my own height, their dark robes draped over a form soft and plump—must have unnerved them, for they said, "Greetings, starlight watcher. I am Ailta, the lastborn of the stars, attendant to Our Queen."

"Uhm." My tongue stuck in my throat. "I'm Sister Elegy, of the Watchful Eyes."

I do remember the light of her smile. The memory is faint, but I have not lost it yet.

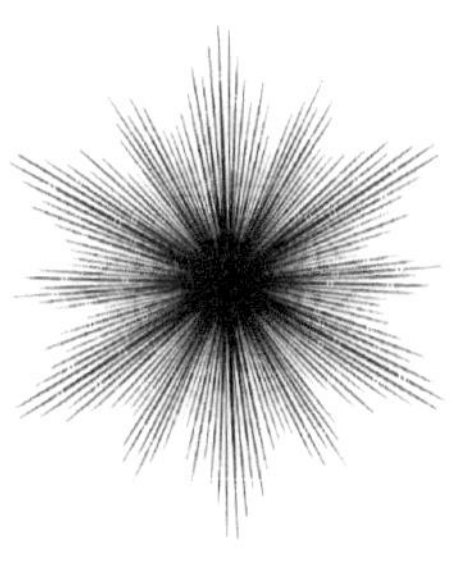

iii.

"I AM NOT MEET TO UNDERTAKE such a journey!"

This burst from me after a long morning in the Starlit Mother's chambers of office. The old woman, the leader of the monastery (and venerable even then), looked up sharply at my exclamation. She was not used to dealing with resistance such as this.

"You are the *only* one meet for such a journey," she responded gently. Her silver clinked in the warm half-light of a morning demanding entry through a tiny, iron-paned window. Her lips were set just as resolutely as that iron. "Though that lies beside the point. It was under your watch that the Queen's Attendant has come, therefore—"

An "augh," burst from me then, cutting her off, as I tried to marshal any argument—any at all—to forestall her cold logic. But none came. I couldn't merely say I *wanted* nothing to do with this: with a legend falling right out of the sky onto my head. The monastic life has little to do with *want*, with desire.

"As I said." This was colder, more demanding. "The Queen must rise, with her hosts."

"I apologize, Starlit Mother," I managed. "It's only—"

"The road will be hard. This I know. Especially as the Capitol is in the midst of a bustling merchant trade. Had I the means, I would send a score to escort such a visitor." Her smile was cruel. "Perhaps, if you could visit another of our Order . . ."

The Starlit Mother spoke this full in jest. Even then, we knew we were the last of this Order; I had never met any Siblings from the other fallen monasteries. We existed in the margins of the world's forgetfulness. We still do, make no mistake.

Thus, the responsibility was ours.

It was mine.

The voice of the Starlit Mother dripped low with sudden mercy. "Do not think I forget your . . . particular position, Sister. Travel light, and keep to the shadows of night."

In the end, I hung my head and accepted my fate. A flash of steel played across my mind. "I accept this road, Starlit Mother."

"Then let the blessing of the stars light your path."

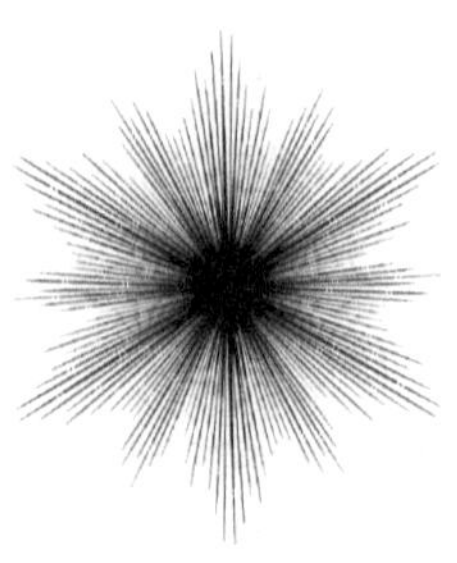

iv.

IT MUST HAVE BEEN THE SAME DAY when I visited our guest; mere hours after she had descended from the starry heavens. It must have . . . but it feels like a conversation out of time, untethered to any moment.

"I am a woman," Ailta said, without any rancor. That mood simply did not exist within her heart; at least, not from what I observed of her. "As are you?"

I don't think this was the beginning of our talk, but it is what I remember first. I nodded and poured her a glass of tea. Orange and sharp. "Our societies have been so long apart. I apologize for the intrusion. I know not your custom."

"It is nothing. What do you know of our . . . society, Sister Elegy?"

The way she spoke my name . . . it made up for the pain through which I had earned it. Well, almost. "We have the *Book of the Queen*. It speaks a few details of your society, of your few kinships."

"Kinships." Ailta laughed. "What, you mean a simple clan or three?"

"Seven, I think it was."

Ailta nodded. "The seven holds, though that has little to do with the day to day anymore. By the Queen's decree, the stars have been fixed in their places, awaiting her return. You are the first person I've spoken to in a long, long time, Sister Elegy."

I blinked. What she spoke rang true—the stars were not wont to scurry helter-skelter across the heavens as people might on Melodia. But it had never occurred to me before this moment . . .

"Does it not grow lonely? I . . . the night sky always seemed so cold, so distant, even as it shone in beauty."

"I was lucky," Ailta said. "The passing moons bring

news across the firmament, the lesser and the greater both in their times decreed. Not that they would converse with a simple star such as I, even an Attendant to our Queen. In the beginning, after all, there were one hundred and forty-four of us. I merely outlived the rest."

She sighed. "But I got used to it, gazing down upon the distant, shining realm below. Through the long watches of night and day, I could not help but observe its people, numberless even beyond the shining stars. To live so briefly, and so brightly, to spark against each other in love, in hate—"

I remember looking again at her smile, being captivated by her lips. It was not proper for me, a sworn sister of the Watchful Eyes, but it was the truth. I do think she recognized my attention, because I remember her preening a little, then asking something of me.

"I . . . what? I am sorry."

"Sister Elegy, what brought you to this monastery?"

My heart sank into darkness. "I . . . no. I apologize, Ailta. But of that I do not speak."

I do not remember how that conversation ended—

only that her eyes bore apology for any harm done to me. I accepted her grace as a Sister must.

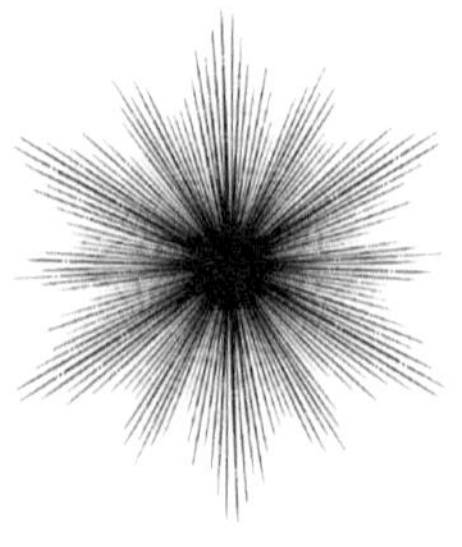

V.

"The Queen stirs."

All the Siblings of the Monastery had gathered beneath the low stone roof of the chapel. Brother Greagor stood by the entrance, the honor guard to the proceedings herein, though I had my doubts whether there was any actual threat of violence.

I stood beside the Starlit Mother, my robes pressed and cleaned for the occasion. Ailta stood on her other side, still gleaming in her light.

It was a week since she had arrived. I think. No longer than two, anyway.

You can read the whole of the ceremony, I think. It was

set down at the founding of the Monastery, at the inscription of the Prayer Book. I remember the Starlit Mother's clear voice, ringing like sunlight across glassy seas. "To her tomb, a star shall go. And by the hand of our best, the star's path should be warded."

I remember this line. It was my cue. I stood and said, "I am unworthy of this calling."

I was not protesting in truth—these were, of course, the words I was meant to say at this time, in this place. Though perhaps I put too much feeling into them, for the Starlit Mother's next line came sharp.

"Then I will *prepare* your worthiness." She stepped forward and announced, "The host of our Queen shall fall from heaven, and reign in glory on this fallen world."

The cup, the sprinkling of lustrated water, and so on. This was one of the High Rites, always prepared for but never performed in living memory. Still, it felt much like any other rite in the sanctuary.

The only difference was Ailta.

I couldn't help but steal looks her way, all through the ceremony. And I certainly was not the only one. A star, come down to our monastery? True, we were the last of our order, a silent sentinel guarding the pass leading through the western peaks. And was it not written that the Queen's holy seekers should reverse the passage of the sun, traveling west to east? So Brother Carl says. Yes, even in my hearing these days. I think he does it to mock me.

Ailta brightened the rite to its conclusion. And before the sun could rest upon the horizon, the two of us had departed with a mule purchased from the little village beside the stream below the Monastery.

Did I believe in all that, then? Of the Queen and the holy seekers? Of her golden host? Of course I did. I drank in the intoxication of the hymns, the joyful declamations, the solemn liturgies. And then, at the apex of my faith, I walked beside a living star fallen from the heavens.

Do I believe now? Honestly, I cannot say.

vi.

OH, I HAD FORGOTTEN. What next I speak occurred before the rite. I am sorry. My memory is not as it once was, you know.

I was set on another vigil, almost a week after Ailta's arrival. It can't have been sooner, as our vigil nights were rotated evenly among all the Watchful Siblings. My mind—well. It feels as if this happened after the rite, but that is impossible.

Ailta was there. She did not have the same need of rest as we Siblings did; she required some, but it was a matter of an hour here and there. Never did it follow true the cycle of the sun.

So her eyes were bright with vigor as she asked, "What are you writing now?"

I looked down at my shorthand. "The rising of Vaiar in the east." I nudged the chronometer. "The red star rises precisely two hours and seventeen minutes after sundown on this night."

"And did it come in on time?"

I smiled to myself. "Well, from this vantage, it was four minutes late. But that is only because Old Tumbledown blocks the view." I gestured to the dark crumple of ancient rock on the horizon, the least picturesque peak I could see.

"Old Tumbledown? And how did such a majestic peak earn that name?"

"I'm . . . not sure I recall." Was it . . . oh, the old story about the goat and the troll? *Tumble down, tumble down, all the way home.* Unconsciously I began humming the old childhood tune. I saw Ailta catch the melody, and as I broke off suddenly, she began singing.

Dear old Tumbledown, hear our charm.
Keep our fathers from all harm.

Keep our mothers in the light.
Let the soldiers sleep tonight.
Let the maidens pine in peace.
Grant our sickly kind release.
And us children, let us play
All throughout the live-long day.

"I . . ." I had, back then, only recalled parts of the rhyme. (*Let us play . . .*) But the star sounded as if she had sung it every night for years. It brought a shiver of unkind memory to me. "Do you often sing such songs, um, above?"

"Oh, only what I hear." Ailta crooked her head. "The songs that rise up through the night."

"You've a skilled singing voice." It was true. Not fit for a bawdy tavern verse, hers. Though she would make even the raunchiest lines utterly lovely. "I've never had the talent."

"Oh, but I love hearing such things! Sung without care, warbled without worry or pretense."

"You'll not get me to sing." I was worried she would, in

fact, get me to sing.

"Well, now that you're all a bundle of worry, why would I ask? No, I'll steal the treasure of your song when it shines without care, without stress."

That made me even more worried. And . . . *treasure of your song*. Damn.

She said that sort of thing all the time.

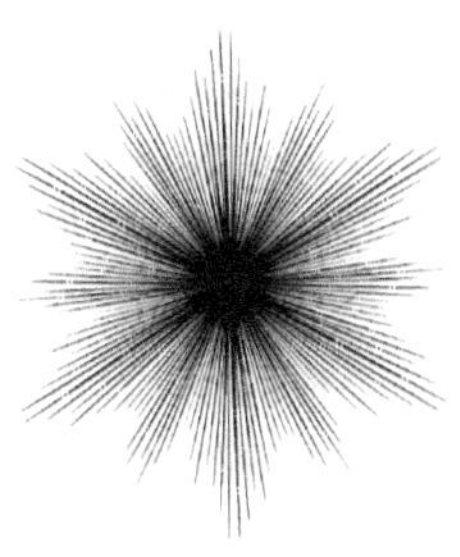

vii.

WHAT ELSE SHOULD I SAY OF the Monastery? It was much as you know it, though I remember it more brightly. The yellow days when Sibling Alden would steep rosemary tea for our high zenith meal; the howling of winter's tenacious hold upon the stone, though the tale of days would have the gall to name it spring; the endless games of Queening played with Dusty; ale in the autumn, roast in the winter, and stolen sips of wine from the storehouse come summer; and you.

Even now, I cannot call this place anything but home. But that is not my story.

I was in my chambers. This was also before the rite.

You know the Monastery takes our worldly possessions—and that is what Brother Greagor always said, "worldly possessions," with all the gravel of a mountain scree—and keeps them against the failure of our Watch. There are some who last only a year, maybe two, among the Watchful Siblings, and so their possessions are returned to them once they leave.

I never expected to see the contents of that tiny box again. It had been, oh, at that point? Twenty years? Something close to that figure, I expect.

Long-dried flowers spilled onto my cot, along with moth-eaten clothes. I held up the traveling dress, the one I wore when first I came to the Monastery. It was faded even then. You know, the Siblings might still have it. Yes, it was worn, but still strong for the journey.

I folded it and, reaching in again, set aside a small pouch from the box. Clinking below it was the final possession I arrived with.

It set my heart pounding. A flash of gleaming steel—

I shook my head, which did a poor job of clearing it.

I pulled out the long knife, a single span of sharpness

above a simple leather-bound hilt. It still shone as brightly as when I had surrendered it, both the polish and the edge undimmed. The simple belt of the same leather lay below it, still attached to the scabbard.

After a moment looking at my reflection in the blade, I placed it gently within the scabbard, and all upon the folded dress. I moved carefully so as not to cut my finger upon it.

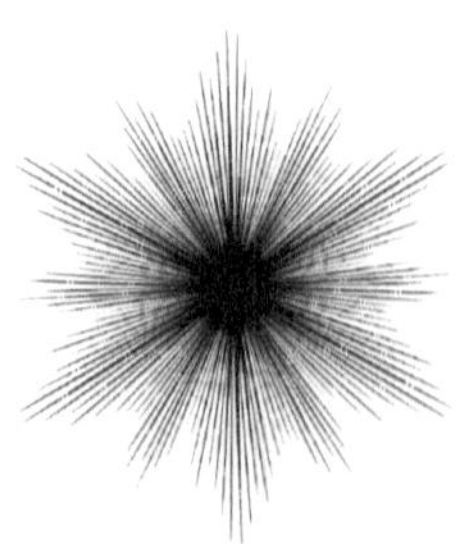

viii.

NO, IT IS NOT YET TIME to speak that rancid tale.

When I left to Ward the path ahead for Ailta, I carried my old knife. That is enough for now.

ix.

IT WAS THREE DAYS SINCE THE START of our journey. We had visited the little village below the Monastery, sleeping through the day and rising with the night. I expected the need for a hooded lantern, to show our way through the dark pass descending to the Capitol. But I needn't have bothered.

Ailta was light enough for us.

She would stretch her hand before her and between her tender fingers a glow of starlight would gather, pure and soft and clear. It was not a light that strained the eyes. No, it wrapped my sight in the velvet of the night, so I began to look upon the unclouded days as harsh and cruel.

But that was our time for sleep, as we passed down the mountain in careful silence.

Those early days we talked much, but those words have long slipped from my memory. Ailta was as she always was. Careful words would strike my heart and linger there long afterwards.

We were in the outlying villages of the Capitol, I recall, when next I remember her voice.

"Warden Elegy,"—for I was no longer a Sister; my calling had changed—"I know so little of your craft."

"My craft?"

"Everyone has a craft," she said, as if it were the most obvious observation below the sea of night. We wandered into the flickering light of an inn, and she extinguished the mote of starlight that had lit our way. "From those who work in metal, to those who work in great columns of numbers. I would watch a person ply their craft for long stretches of my vigil. What is yours?"

I swallowed. I could not tell her, not then. Not there. "I had little time for craft as I grew out of childhood. I was …" I paused, wondering how close I should skirt the truth.

"The affairs of a noble House leave little time for such diversions."

"Oh, but that is the most subtle of crafts!" We were now seated at a table, and I still remember the ale-drenched smell of the wood. Our stew was served once I passed a few shining copper Capitols to the serving-boy. Ailta's eyes were shining as she spoke. "When done poorly, all around suffer. But when plied well, the land flourishes."

That had not been my experience. What one noble Laird would consider good governance would differ much from the opinions of those under rule. And chance and the seasons could ruin both the just and unjust. But I was diplomatic. "There is a balance one must strike, and sometimes such a tightrope is difficult for even the most accomplished statesman to walk unmarred."

Ailta nodded sagely. "I think the motive force of a noble House can be difficult to arrest."

Well, that was true.

We tucked into our meal. It was halfway through my stew that I heard Ailta take in a sudden breath. I looked up sharply, but fear was not on her features—only surprise.

"There are a few who seek us," she said. At this, fear tensed through my arms, and my fingers went directly to the long knife. Ailta cocked her head. "Oh, dear. They mean to kill you, I believe."

I swore. Had I not been careful in my travel? I drew the hood back over my head. I had begun to take for granted Ailta's abilities by this point—her eyes and other senses could pierce far beyond what mortals ever could. My mind whirred along pathways I had long thought far behind me. But, when once you wield a blade . . .

"Come," I said, pushing away the remains of my stew. "We must fly. From whence are they approaching?"

"Through the front, I think. They're not very devious, I must say." Ailta's face still carried none of the fear that coursed through my blood. But I was her Warden, so she rose and followed me as I pushed through the taproom and through the door to the kitchens.

Was there a commotion as we pressed through to the dark alley beyond? I would imagine so, but the vision in my memory narrows to a point sharper than a needle. We made it to the alley, and our eyes adjusted quickly to the night. I'd like to thank Ailta for that—she warded me far better than I her.

"What are they saying?" I had heard the crash of the front door slamming inward, but the admixture of voices at that distance made it impossible for me to hear their words.

"They seek . . . yes, they seek you? By order of the local governor. Oh, this is a story you must share with me, Warden Elegy."

I would not share that story for a little while. We slipped down the alley, and nearly made good our escape. But those hunting me were smarter than Ailta had assumed.

Two soldiers, I recall. The trick to killing swordsmen with a knife is this: strike before they can unsheathe. A swift cut to the throat, and I recall only the dark blood pooling at my feet, but I did not pause before slicing the other soldier across the neck. She dropped her hand crossbow, a weapon I considered far more deadly than the blade, and joined her comrade in death.

I pulled the two cooling corpses into the darkest corner

of the alleyway and stowed the crossbow in my pack. With a nod to Ailta, we hurried away. I sheathed my blade without cleaning it.

We were in the fields outside the town before I felt I could catch my breath. I sat down, leaned against a fence-post, and Ailta was beside me.

"So that is your craft," she said. Her eyes must have held disappointment, though I heard none in her voice. "I've seen many ply the trade of death, but your movements were deft even compared to theirs."

"We should stay off the roads until the country is much changed," I managed. "It is my fault, not yours. I am a poor choice for a Warden."

Ailta protested, but it was the truth.

X.

WE PASSED THROUGH THE RIVER that night, as I was suspicious that hounds would soon pick up our trail. How they would distinguish our scent among all the other guests of the inn that night, I did not know. But it paid to be cautious.

I have little memory of the country surrounding the Capitol. We were being pursued, but our lead grew longer as we ascended from the valley and into the wide plain. Ailta was unused to fear—in all my time with her, she never shared with me a terrified glance, nor a frightful whisper. She explained this in the hours before one grey dawn.

"This body is but a cage for me. One that I must wear

if my duty to the Queen would be fulfilled—I cannot awaken her and bring down her hosts in spirit only. But should this hot blood spill from me, I would simply ascend, once more, into the sea above."

"So why would your path need *me* to ward it?"

"There are few times I can descend again. Should this mortal form perish on the journey, I could only return after twenty-nine more years of the Sun. Elsewise, the barrier between my sea and yours fixes me in place. And still, the Queen would sleep."

By the Queen's decree, yes. I closed my eyes, but only the flash of steel awaited me in my dreams. And my brother. Oh yes, his face I remember well.

The land that rolled before us was wide and beautiful under starlight, under the phases of the moons violet and silver. That I cannot deny.

XI.

This tale grows long in the telling, and I am sick at heart. I must tell you of something beautiful, I think. Something golden. Were I a better . . . no. I will not apologize for my lack of craft. Only I can tell this story to you. And I thank you—coming to me here, in this pit, to listen.

The truest prison is to be forgotten.

I must reckon time again. Another month had passed, for summer was drawing long. Things happened between us, yes; important things that you must know, but to those I will turn later. For now, know that we had passed the river and evaded pursuit. The valley was behind us, the wide plain ahead, and a nearby village waited. Farming country.

We would need to pass at a greater sea beneath a sharp grin of towering mountains before our journey was done.

We chanced awakening before the sun had set—hours before. Our schedule had fallen out of balance. Ailta had grown cold to me, though she yet thanked me for my watch, as was her waking habit.

The fields, heavy with grain, swayed in a light breeze.

"The harvest will soon begin," she said as she braided together a handful of long, wild grasses. "Oh, I cannot count the cycles of the sun I have seen. How many have you?"

"Sorry?"

"How old are you? Oh, if I'm being rude, I apologize. But in years . . . these are the rhythm of my life, above. How many have you seen?"

"Years?" I considered. And now, let me think again. How many had passed in my life before we met? It must have been no less than thirty-four, if my counting is right. I think I told her the truth.

I remember she nodded. "The year, it always goes the same. From deathly cold to naked heat, and back again. The dance . . ."

"We must press on," I said. I was thankful to walk below the sun once more, but my place was as her Warden. I knew she must want to visit the village. To see a festival, and move among it as she never could above. By the Queen, I wanted that too. But as her Warden . . .

"No," I added. "I don't know if we are still being pursued. But the risk, if we are . . ."

"I recall what you said about yourself." Her wide eyes were on me, serious enough that I knew she understood the risks well herself. She put a hand on my shoulder. "But I would not have you shatter further. Can we not rest, and have to ourselves a little amusement?"

I blinked. I don't think I remembered, in that instant, what she referred to, but it came back to me quickly. *Shatter . . .*

You will understand this when I find the courage to speak of Ailta's glass, of what had passed between us a week or so before. She was being kind, and speaking with more feeling than she had the days gone past. I apologize, for I cannot speak of that now. I must gather my strength for it.

I looked across the fields to the gathering of buildings that made the nearby village, joined in a circle on a gentle sweeping rise. Below the dusky sky, I could believe the village itself would dance. A fine harvest was coming in, with the promise of food and life even though, as the year drew quickly on, the winter snows would fain snuff that warmth away. For now, the village would dance and feast.

How much more would they feast when the Queen came in her glory? I wonder even now.

But still . . .

"We are strangers here."

"Wherever I go, I am a stranger." There was a sadness in her voice, one I felt I could not abide.

I drew in a breath, heart rising to my throat. "Well, not to me, you aren't."

Ailta drew in a quick breath, and I caught her eyes. They glimmered in her starlight. And . . .

Oh, by the Queen . . .

Yes, hold! But for a moment. I recall her . . . Hold! Please, I beg you. *I cannot lose it now!*

Okay. Thank you. I—yes. A moment more, if you

would.

I'm alright.

Thank you. No, take it. I'd only stain it further.

Under the golden light of the setting sun, yes, that is right. The night of the festival. If only I could *show* it to you. Her silver hair. Her nose, sharp like the darting of a rabbit through a bush. Those full, teardrop cheeks. And her *smile*.

Oh, I recall what I thought lost forever on the dark sea of memory.

I finally remember her face.

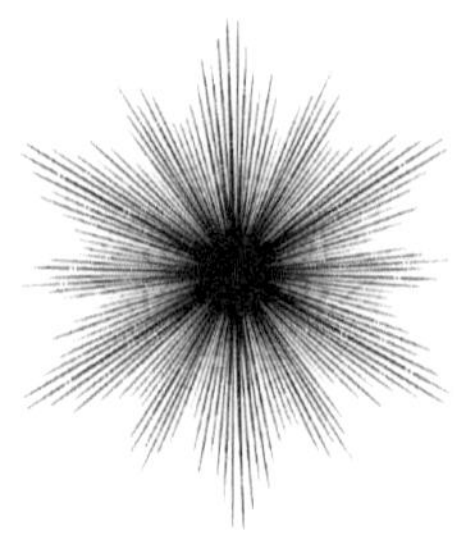

xii.

THIS STORY WOULD BREAK ME if it could. Happiness, joy? They carve deeper wounds than you know. Though I'm glad of the telling, in the end. And it must be done.

Why must memories fade?

The village, then.

We wandered into the village square after a quarter hour, and saw the villagers had long concluded their feast. The golden hour was here, the sun barely dipping beyond the now-distant line of purple mountains to our back. I was being led by Ailta, my mind still distracted, thinking on the look she'd given me back at the road. I'd only spoken the truth . . .

She was no stranger to me.

So I blinked and it seemed that the barn appeared before me as if conjured from the dust of the village. The door to it hung ajar. I looked at Ailta.

"The villagers dress in masks, you see." She pointed down to the square. "Should we wish to celebrate with them, we must look the part."

I put my arm on her shoulder as she moved to pull me into the barn. "We shouldn't."

"We steal nothing but a night with these unused masks," Ailta said. And then, looking in my eyes, she said what I've taken as a proverb all these long nights since.

"Many are the doors that should be unlocked, and are not. Few there are that should be locked, and are not."

I looked at her in disbelief. "Are you being serious? Many are . . . that's ridiculous."

"And anyway, this door is yet unlocked. Come!"

I let her lead me into the barn. Left strewn across the haybales were several masks—demonic things. I think you've seen the woodcuts from Sibling Alden. Perfect terrors for a village festival.

Mine was scratchy with hay, but I wore it. Ailta was a tidy storm, buffeting me through the door of the barn and out into the golden hour again. We faded into the crowd of villagers as we approached the bonfire.

"I never understood this part," Ailta whispered. She was clutching my arm, now, and I could hear her smile. She'd picked my mask, and took a little satisfaction in it.

"The . . ." I looked at the bonfire, and the man of straw being paraded before it. "Oh, John Barleycorn. Though they might have their own name for him."

"Yes, I think further east they name him Ivan. Which is just John by another tongue."

"How much can you hear of us so far above Melodia, sailing through your sea of night?"

"I hear enough." Again, I clearly heard her smile. "But," she continued, the smile gone for but a moment, "the burning of him. I don't understand."

"Well, he's the symbol of the harvest." I cast my mind back to my lessons, long before the monastery. My mother taught me all the common festivals, which didn't please my father much, I think. "The harvest has, until now, grown up in full life. But now it must perish, and by perishing, support the village through a long winter. So, the village takes responsibility for it, I suppose. You never heard the song?"

"Sing it for me." She had not given up on her private campaign to get me to sing. But thankfully, the village headswoman saved me and gestured for all the village to sing—as if to prove my point exactly.

John Barleycorn must die . . .

Oh, what else can I tell you? After the village joined in song, there was a whirl of dancing, of laughing, of the freshest ale newly brewed for the occasion. All these mix together in a whirling storm of sweetness—of Ailta. She was that storm, yes. And, my little storm, she carried me laughing through the night.

I didn't understand it then, the significance of that song. I don't think I ought to have taught it to her, after.

xiii.

Yes, it has been a while. I am sorry.

But I think I do have strength enough to speak what I passed over last time.

Just give me patience? Of course.

Well, it's not like I'm going anywhere.

This would have been a week before the festival I spoke of. No more than two. And only that long since we had escaped the governor's men. When I had drawn and bloodied my knife, yes.

I do not regret that, no. I was her Warden. Those two I killed do not weigh upon my conscience.

We were traveling by night, as I said before. Well, we

did then, before the festival. Afterwards, well, I let down my guard. But let me focus on the story at hand.

The soldiers from the governor were not letting up on us. Passing through the river kept them from us for a night or two, but we needed to avoid the roads, you understand. Our progress was slow. Sometimes we would hit upon a trail that led more or less towards our goal. But the forests were becoming rarer, the land flatter. A pursuer need not catch us in the undergrowth of the old oak, when he knew we were heading east.

We passed miles south of the Capitol. I was sad to let it go by. I think one night, just after dusk but before I awoke Ailta, I stood on a rise looking north, trying to pick out which lights on the horizon belonged to the Capitol, and which belonged to . . .

No. I must focus.

I tell my tale in my own way, and in my own time. I imagine this makes it more difficult for you, but it is the only way I can.

It was that night—the night I picked out the lights of the Capitol—when I noticed, at first, the working in Ailta's hands.

She wasn't keeping it secret, but she wasn't making a show of it either. I would glance back and see a silver fire dance between her fingers, see it glinting across a thousand tiny facets caught in her hand. At first, I thought she'd caught an orb of starlight. But with every backward glance, I realized what it was.

A masterpiece in glass.

She was whispering to it as we walked. She'd put it away when we needed to climb over difficult tangles of roots, to wade through a stream, or to do anything more strenuous. But every time we found a trail, or we left the cover of trees for the open night above, she pulled it from her satchel and continued her work.

I never got a good look at it, not at that time. And a few nights passed this way. Oh, yes, we'd talk. I don't recall what about. Whispered conversation, her eyes wide and taking in the world up close one blink at a time. But she knew when to keep quiet, which made my job as Warden that much easier.

On the third night, probably an hour after sundown, I

walked right into the bounty hunter's blade.

Ailta started as the man, clad all in black, stepped from his hiding place under the bush. His blade was at my throat. My eyes went back to the star, and saw her quickly stow that thing of glass and starlight in her pouch. Her hands were up in an instant, right where the soldier could see them.

The man nodded. "Well," he said, and the way he said it stuck in my memory. It was the dry, toneless "well" of letting someone through the city gates after a glance at their papers. It was the tuneless "well" of a mother told of her children fighting for the twentieth time. It was the type of "well" that came from a man about to string up a lucrative bounty—though, perhaps, the third this week.

Oh, no, not the star. Me.

"Keep your hands up," he said in that same low tone. He pulled out a folded poster, then held it up to my face. "Your nose is different, yeah?"

"They've never been able to capture it," I said. I angled my head. "How about now?"

"What are you *doing*?" The star had her hands over her

mouth, her eyes not quite certain if they should be fearful.

"Just making a living." I'll give the bounty hunter this. He took the question in stride as he stripped my knife from its sheath, throwing it down and away from the three of us. "Your friend is wanted by Sir Titus Delacore, the governor of this province. And to the tune of sixteen hundred Republic Crowns, well, I'd say he bloody well gets what he wants."

"It's been nearly twenty years," I said. More to myself than the bounty hunter, really.

"Well, that's between you and the governor, miss. I'm just the one after the reward. You understand."

Ailta moved then, darted towards the bounty hunter, but the man was quick with his blade. He swiveled and nearly impaled the star, who instinctively jumped back half an inch. "Ah! Good try, I'll admit. Trying to get in my blind spot and all. Now, keep your hands where I can see them."

But his eyes had left my form for a few seconds too long. It was distraction enough.

I slammed my fist into his shoulder, sending him off balance. Then, I swept his legs—and I will also admit, I remember his stance was firm. It nearly didn't work. The flash of adrenalin at failure kicked through my abdomen.

I followed up with another punch to his back, and then a knee lower down. It was enough. He tumbled, and my fingers were quick. His hands went directly to his belt—his instincts were good.

His blade was already in my hand. And I swung as surely and as mechanically as I ever did cutting wood for the monastery.

A flash of red. His hand knocked against the nearby tree. Three fingers spun away, trailing blood.

And Ailta screamed.

The bounty hunter's blade was now at his own throat. He quivered under the pain of losing digits. They were from his left hand, but I suspect he prized them all the same.

"Now, what should I do with you?"

Oh, my voice was much colder than it is now. I don't think I can replicate it well. Hm. Cold, ruthless. Like the calm smoothness of a frozen lake.

Stop laughing. This is serious!

No. If you can't respect my tale, then it shall have to wait.

xiv.

Hey, watch who you're calling an old woman. Do you want to hear it, or not?

Well, alright then.

Yes, I remember where I left off. Fingers flying through the air. Those words which came to my lips as easy as a smile, but not half so comforting. "Now, what should I do with you?"

Ailta's eyes were wide, refracting starlight through tears. "No . . ." she said faintly.

And the bounty hunter picked up on that. "You don't have to—I have a family, you know. Two little boys—"

"You. Quiet." I had my doubts. Well, it wasn't so unthinkable. *Someone* could have loved his face long enough to pull off such a feat as a child. Even twice.

I closed my eyes for half a second, then opened them and prodded the bounty hunter in the neck again, in case he got ideas. Then, I looked across to Ailta. "You must understand; yes, this is my fault, but I cannot protect you if I let one such as this walk free."

Ailta's eyes were hard. "We can fly faster than this one could ever scurry after. Especially since he'd need to head to the village an hour west to see to his wounds. We'd outpace him easily."

The bounty hunter agreed vigorously, though quietly, with this assessment. And . . . well, Ailta did have a point.

You know this wouldn't be the last time I let my frustration cloud my judgment. Right, like you haven't either.

"I'll keep your weapons," I said shortly. The bounty hunter nodded, then stripped two of the knives from his sleeves and dropped them on the ground. This one took initiative. Not common among his kind.

"And empty out your boots. If you don't have a knife down each, then you deserved to lose those fingers."

"Oh," Ailta said. I looked up at her, but she shook her head. Mere surprise graced her eyes. And the ghost of gratitude.

Sure enough, two tiny blades fell from his black boots. They were good boots, well-cured leather. I considered keeping them, but they weren't my size anyway.

Ailta had taken the bounty hunter's hand and wrapped the stumps in a steadily reddening cloth. "Thank ye," he said, but the star said nothing to him. Her eyes were on me. Though I couldn't guess why. I'd given her what she wanted, after all.

After a minute, he had staggered off into the forest behind us, and I had gathered what I wanted to keep from his weapons—just the long blade, which could be useful to wear and ward off the more cowardly kind of bandit. I hadn't trained with such a weapon, but I could use it in a pinch. I'd keep my knife beside it, after all.

But then Ailta surprised me. She held out a hand for the blade, and I gave it her.

She was not built for fighting. Hiking, sure. She would lose her breath after a good uphill stretch, but she kept pace with me reasonably well for one who had not inhabited a mortal body for untold ages of the world. But the smoothness of her skin, of her fingers—the weight that graced her form—spoke not of the training needed for a fighter.

But she held the blade in a practiced grip. She took a few swings, and I judged them for myself. "Good," I found myself saying, before I could help it. She smiled at me, and it only seemed a little forced.

Then, we headed down the trail once more, together.

No, I'm not done for the night. What do you mean, I'm always so short? I take just as long as I need to.

Well, with that attitude, *now* I might be done.

I thought so!

"I see many things about you," the star began, a few minutes down the road. "The way you hold the knife, it fits into your grip like the hand of a lover. You *dance* with it, or the movement of your arm looks so."

"Dance?"

The star shook her head. "I'm still in awe of how a body moves, and there is little of the way you move I cannot fail to find wonder in. And the way the knife's weight balances against your grip . . ." She shuddered, a mixture of terror and surprise quivering in her eyes. "Where did you learn to do that? To dance your arm while gripping steel?"

I stopped. My hand made a go of reaching for that very knife, but I arrested it. It quivered, and I realized I had missed the weight of steel. Even after all this time . . . after what such weight had bought me . . .

"I will tell you," I said. "But not tonight. Tonight is grim and bloody enough as it is."

A glimmer of glass disappeared into the star's pack. "I trust you, Sister Elegy." This was spoken not as a warning, but as a simple fact. "Such dances of steel are not to my liking, but they have their place."

XV.

It must have been the very next night when she said, "I have something for you."

I remember I was looking to the sky at that moment. My idle thoughts had turned to where this particular star, Ailta, had been placed within the heavens. In fact, I believe I had opened my mouth to voice this question when she spoke first.

"I . . . um." I looked over to the star. She wasn't holding anything surprising—the glimmer of starlit glass in her palm, refracting like the surface of a brilliantly-cut gem. But she held it in both hands now, and those hands approached me.

I reached out one of my own tentatively. I wondered if my earthly fingers would dispel the light.

Ailta placed a globe the size of my fist into my palm. The surface was smooth glass, or perhaps some sort of crystal. It was heavier than it looked. And within . . .

A dance. Starlight spun along long pathways of cracks carefully introduced through the globe, shimmering and refracting and making a miniature of the night sky, if the stars above could sway and streak across the heavens far more freely.

A thought came to me then. I nearly opened my mouth to voice it, but it didn't seem the right time.

I looked up into Ailta's face. Oh, the memory of her face is so real in my mind, so . . . I feel I could touch it as surely as I touch yours. I could pinch it and fold it up and stow it in my pocket . . .

How did I ever forget?

"What is it?"

My thanks were trampled by my curiosity, but Ailta didn't seem to mind. "It is starlight. A little of my own, and I shaped the glass from some I . . . well, Dusty gave me a tumbler of glass my first night, something from his grandmother.”

“And you . . . shaped it?” I recall the glassblowers in the market, and once I was allowed in to see them work. The process requires great heat, as much as any blacksmith’s forge. “How?”

“Through starlight.” She did not elaborate.

My thanks caught up, then, late as usual. “I’m . . . this is beautiful, and I thank you for the gift, but—”

“You are my Warden. Your daily duty performed so freely on my behalf is thanks enough.”

She was very close to me, then. I could smell the breath of heaven on her lips. But I closed my eyes and pulled back. “I don’t . . .”

“What is it?”

“I don’t deserve this.” My hand holding the globe of starlight fell to my side, and I nearly dropped her gift upon the ground. I changed my grip.

“I decide this, not you. This is *my* gift.” An edge of frustration crept into her voice, and I saw her eyes sharpen.

“Well, I suppose you should decide.” That was only

fair, I thought. We continued walking along the fenced-in field, the stars of Ailta's sea above giving ample light to our path.

And I spoke. I spoke the story of my youth, before I first came to the monastery.

The same story I will now tell to you.

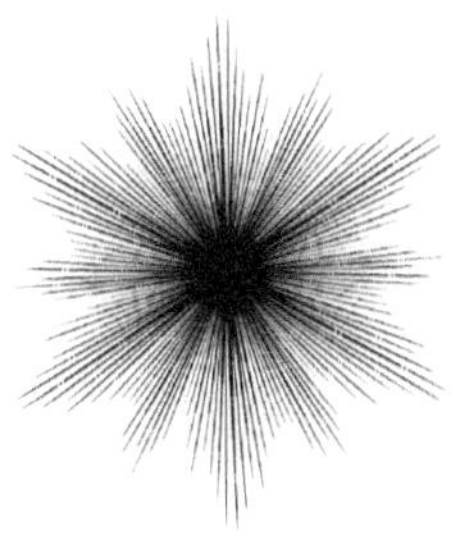

XVI.

I WAS NOBLE BORN.

Oh, I will not speak the name of my Father's house. If you wish, you can consult the records in the Capitol. Nothing there is kept hidden. Most of what I tell you has been publicly recorded, kept by the officers of the courts at the time. They will know me by my chosen name.

I was not the firstborn of that house. Nor was I the second; that was my brother, Marten, who became the heir after my eldest sister passed from a bout of cholera. She was five years old, and I was but a babe.

I knew her only from a painting hanging in my parents' quarters. Her lips were closed, and she stood in a meadow.

She wasn't smiling, but her eyes followed any who entered the room. In the days of my childhood, I was afraid of her.

But childhood passed into adolescence, and my training drove all fear from me.

Marten would be the heir. This was before the appointment of the governor, before the election of the general assembly. Our little republic is small among the wider world of Melodia, but it has seen much hardship at the hands of the nobility.

I was taught to master my fear. But I think my Father never did. He was cruel towards the peasants on our land. *Our* land, I was taught. And so it was. Though we did not have the care or keeping of it.

Oh, I speak from long experience that I was not blessed with at the time. Long bitterness, nurtured here in my cell. Back then, I knew only Father, Mother, and Marten. I was the third born, and the keeping of my brother was my responsibility.

I learned the use of herbs for poison and for dispelling the same. I learned the affairs of the state, of the crown we must bow to in the Capitol, of the other noble houses arranged neatly beneath it. I learned our true enemies were these other noble houses. They would stoop as a falcon in flight to snatch our land, our titles. The peasants must be kept in line, yes; but our true rivals were those the crown named as our equals.

Our peers.

And so I also learned the blade. I grew to love my brother, as the knight grows to love her liege. He was the reason I existed. In him were all the hopes of our House placed.

As I said before, the trick to killing swordsmen with a knife is this: strike before they can unsheathe. I learned a more general rule: strike before I could be seen, by any means at my disposal. The unknown killer is always more dangerous than the known.

The other noble Houses well learned that lesson, too.

Should I speak of our House? Of the mahogany steps that led to our shared bedroom? Of the winter nights spent shivering with my brother before the roaring fire, and our Nan reading dark stories of the frozen East to terrify and comfort? Of the endless drills, the presentations given before Father in perfect recitation, the falconer I spied going to and fro in the woods of our estate—the envy I held of his freedom, his skill with the bird? And a hundred other tiny things: fresh apples in summer, ale for the harvest, and the wide, hungry mouth of clear skies threatening to swallow me and Marten up?

Yes, this was as much my home as the monastery. And I carry it with me every day.

I was fourteen when it ended.

The general alarm rose above the House one morning. It started a drumbeat in my heart. Father had gone to the Capitol, and Mother had followed a few days later. We were alone . . . vulnerable. Nan rushed into our room to warn us, but I was already in place, blade already held between any enemy and Marten. She rushed out again; I have never seen her among the living since.

Marten was named well—for he was my bird, trained up and ready to be loosed upon the other Houses when he came of age. But for now, we were both chicks. He was not defenseless, but his studies were of matters of state, of grand strategy, of taxation and mercantile affairs. And he had taken to them naturally; for I was his blade. His body was given unto me for safekeeping.

The door was locked. I heard the cry of soldiers defending and dying for our House far below in the courtyard. There was no window, and only a tiny, claustrophobic passage led secretly away into the forest, promising an hour of climbing through the dark and dirt and roots and spiders.

Soon enough, I heard the cry from the courtyard.

"Surrender! We have the head of your treasonous House!"

We heard the soldiers of our house surrendering. I couldn't help but picture it in my mind's eye—my Father's head upon a pike, the soldiers sworn to him throwing down their swords.

They would come for the heir.

Marten was sixteen, two years my elder. And I saw the fear in his eyes.

They would not leave him alive. And could we escape? The long wilderness would not bring any comfort, any respite. And how might we seek safety among those peasants on our land? They would kill us in a moment if they knew who we were. I remember their cruel eyes, the fires burning there.

No, our lives had come to their end.

Marten gently grabbed for the arm that held my blade. I knew him well enough to read his plea.

End it. Please.

My knife could be far more comforting than the cruelties of invading soldiers. I think I remember the stamp of booted feet coming through the house. My grip on the leather was sure, precise.

I placed the point above his heart. It would only be a little pain.

Oh, Marten. I remember his easy smile as he played the fairy courtier on Midwinter Night. His brows would knot when recalling my favorite bird, or reciting another dry fact from his endless history lessons. He would play Queening with me, as Dusty would later. He let me win more often than not.

My blade slid home. I saw the light leave his eyes.

No, it's okay. You needed to know this. As did Ailta.

Later, I was taken into custody of the crown. It was my

blade that had severed the last of my House, and so I faced the punishment of the damned, the fate of the fratricide.

But the crown was merciful. Not the hangman's rope for me. Banishment. Sent to live out the rest of my days in a distant monastery to a nearly forgotten faith, kept just in sight but out of mind.

I was never to leave. And I would not have—had duty not come for me again.

Oh yes. I can see it on your face. Yes, I deserve these irons; in some measure at least.

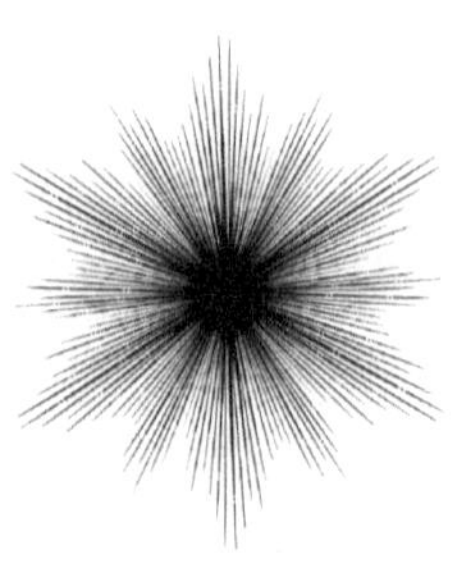

XVII.

AILTA WAS SILENT FOR A LONG TIME after I told that story. Yes, this was the same night as when she gave me that globe of starlight. We had plenty of time to talk. I probably told it better to her; it was fresher in my mind, then, and many details have fled from me since.

The story had given me distraction, and my grip upon her starry globe had slackened. "I do not deserve your kind attention, Ailta." My voice was gentle. "Were it not for my duty to you, I should be shut up in the monastery, living out the punishment for the blood that stains my hands."

"Those same hands defend me, keep me from all harm." Her eyes were hard, insistent. How could I make them understand?

"As they must! But they are not deserving—oh!"

The masterpiece of glass slipped from my fingers. I saw it fall, hitting a wide, flat rock in the path. The starlight scattered as the glass splintered into a thousand, tiny shards. I felt Ailta cry out, saw her reach in vain for the dying lights upon the ground.

"No!" She fell to her knees and wept. Great streaks of tears carved down her cheeks.

I don't remember what I said, then. Perhaps I didn't say anything. My heart had gone out, stopped utterly at the sound of her wretched sobs. Her hands scrabbled across the ground, gathering fragments of the glass even as her shoulders shook.

After a poisoned moment, I gingerly knelt down and helped her. I saw the task as futile—who wouldn't?—but that wasn't the point.

"I'm sorry," I must have said. Ailta shook her head. She didn't look at me. How could she?

I had held a wonder of the world in my palm, a craft of those who swim the ancient sea above. And my carelessness had broken it.

I have long grown bitter from the toxin of that night. Ailta held out a tiny sack, and I poured in the few bloody shards I'd managed to scrape from the dust of the road. "I'm sorry," I repeated. I thought of holding her, of wiping away the tears. But I had no right.

Fixing something is much harder than making something. Even you must understand this? But I think I should have tried.

I spoke once more, a low and sour note that I thought she could not hear. But her ears must have caught it.

"Am I not a broken thing, too?"

xviii.

After that night came the evening we danced at the village festival, as I've told before. Well, yes, of course she had the glass fragments when we went to the festival. I didn't mention it because it wasn't the right time.

We traveled a few weeks more. All pursuit had given up on us by that point. The kingdoms of the plain passed us by in concert with the gentle, steady movement of the moons. Day by day, we drew closer to the wide inner sea. Upon its southern shore rose the Tower of the Queen. One day, there we were.

No, that Tower is not her burial place. Queenscairn still lay a few days ahead, up a steep pass through the mountains. But this was an important stop on Ailta's pilgrimage nonetheless.

I don't recall her task exactly. She needed to find a key, or something like that, long buried beneath the Tower. We rooted through half-collapsed rooms for most of the night until Ailta found what she needed. We took too long for us to continue on the road, so Ailta suggested climbing the Tower and taking our rest there.

Why not? I thought. I wondered if the Queen would use this Tower once more; if it would become a fortress for her conquering hosts. It was an idle thought.

Oh, yes, I believe in my own fashion. Even great Adonai, long dead, could not command so innumerable a host as your Queen.

She is mine no longer.

Blasphemy? I don't know why you're so surprised. What else would you expect from the monastery's prisoner?

Will you let me continue? Oh, how gracious.

The steps upward were steep and unforgiving, but the view as the night faded into dawn at the Tower's pinnacle has stayed in my memory clear and crisp. Ailta's silhouette against the eastern horizon—sorry. There are few mornings when that image doesn't come to my mind's eye unbidden.

"I hate you," she said.

Those words have burned their way upon my heart, too. I didn't think too highly of myself then, but still, they took me aback. "What?"

Ailta's eyes burned as she looked at me, bearing the last remains of bitter tears—though she'd given no indication before. She'd hidden it well.

"How can I not?" Ailta continued as she leaned against the low stone railing, and I realized how high above the plain we really were.

I put my hand on her shoulder, worried for her balance. "Come away from the edge," I said, but she turned and pushed my hand from her. Then, haltingly, I said, "Why . . . do you hate me?"

Ailta turned from me. She picked a spot near the center of the Tower to sit down. I saw her shoulders shake, and she wiped tears from her eyes. "It's . . . I don't know if I can say it well."

I sat beside her. I reached out a tentative hand to wipe the tears from her cheek. She leaned into the touch, which sent a tingle to the back of my head. She grabbed my hand gently, and then said, "I *chose* you. You weren't picked by happenstance. I looked upon your monastery, among those who would honor my vows and Ward my path—and I chose *you*. Because . . ." And at this, she covered her eyes as she began to sob again.

I awkwardly put my arm around her shoulder, and made small sounds of comfort—as a mother might do for her child, perhaps. "It's okay."

"But it's not! I look upon you and I see . . . oh. I see beauty, and grace, and someone worthy of all the honors of this world. And yet, within you is a deeply festering hatred for yourself. How could I not hate you? You bear nothing but loathing for someone I cannot help but lo—"

"I don't des—"

"Bullshit!" Ailta's eyes strove in fiery anger. "You'd just lost your *entire family*. Should someone walk the path of fire after a single mistake in the wake of that loss?"

I was silent, then. Her words, as I said, had a way of resounding with the very beating of my heart. I felt my own tears coming, but I headed them off.

"Perhaps. You might be right. But I've . . ." My words were halting, slow. "I've felt the pain of it every day. Though it stings less, now."

Ailta was breathing heavily, her tears spent. She looked up at me, her eyes pleading. "I thought it would be different. This journey."

I held my breath, wondering . . . wishing . . .

"Different, how?"

I realized how close she was to me, her breath upon my cheek. My arm was still around her, and I felt acutely the warmth of her skin beneath my palm. Her hand came up and caressed the back of my neck—

Our lips met. I can still taste the salt of tears on them.

xix.

After we rested atop the Tower—

What? No, of course not! You think you're entitled to every moment of my life? Let me keep a few private in my heart, will you?

What do you think happened next?

Right. I thought so.

We awoke with the dusk as the first stars were appearing in the east above the mountains. Ailta still looked distant in waking, but she smiled as I caressed her shoulders—

Oh, grow up.

Fine. You win.

After we were fully clothed, *thank you*, I saw her looking out into the sea of night.

"Do you know many of these stars?" I realized she hadn't spoken much at all of her time above. Apart from her loneliness at being fixed in place, I knew little of her past.

"Knew them," Ailta said. My eyes narrowed as she continued. "It's . . . well. I think I'm among the last living stars. Perhaps a hundred more still live, like me."

"I thought—"

"I serve my Queen. But it is not natural for a star to be fixed in place, for ages uncounted! Oh, I've said I had gotten used to it, and that is mostly true . . ." She let out a long breath through her nose. "But that sea is a graveyard. The Queen's decree was our slow death."

"The Queen relied—relies—on a living star to waken her."

"Yes. A single, solitary living star. Our natural lives far exceed any human's, but they don't extend forever. Even if we were allowed to move and—and breathe, and live, and, and . . ."

I put my arm around her, a move already infinitely more familiar and natural than even twelve hours before. "I

. . . well, you know. I've felt the pain of loss, too."

Ailta leaned into me. "It feels . . . there's just this utter emptiness, this void within my heart. Should I mourn them? I have, for the thousands of years I've kept my silent vigil. Even so, some years it felt that I was dead, and only looking through frozen eyes upon a realm below that had forgotten me. Forgotten us."

"I know that feeling. Though perhaps not on the same . . . scale." Being lost . . . being forgotten . . . it may sound comforting until it becomes your living truth. I looked out upon the night sky, a familiar sight to any Watchful Sibling like myself. But now the vista seemed cold and distant.

I thought of the Queen's host, one promised long before the calamity which consumed her world. "What of her armies?" I said. "Surely even She cannot take our world with a bare hundred living stars."

Ailta shook her head. "She would gift those dead with a form of life. But only a form, a . . . muddied reflection."

This disturbed me more than anything else I knew of the Queen. There was a long silence as I pondered. My heart raced, and I felt my mind on the edge of ripping apart, shorn along two diverging paths—

Please. Listen to my words, if ever you have.

Ailta spoke again.

"Some few stars around me still survive," she said. She pointed to a corner of the sky just above the eastern mountains. "There was my appointed place, and . . ."

And then from her I learned the names of those stars fixed beside her. Her place was nearly in the paths of the moons and sun, celestial bodies that still had some life in them, she said. Contact with them, while brief, had kept her living through the ages.

We descended the Tower after an hour or so. Our path ahead wended its way through the foothills on the eastern side of the inner sea, before it rose to the challenge of surmounting the pass.

"You are no soldier," I said after a mile on the road. "Would you return there after your duty is done? Back to your fixed place in the sea above?"

Ailta's eyes were wide. "What choice do I have?"

"Well . . . if you could beg leave of your Queen . . . and stay a while with me . . ."

XX.

One Day More and We Had Surmounted the pass leading to the eastern mountain wilderness. Only half a day's travel lay between us and Queenscairn—so named as it was her final resting place. As her instructions were clear, recorded in the *Book of the Queen*, the tomb was sealed without so much as an honor guard to stand watch over it through the ages.

The alpine air was doing me some good as we rested from the climb through the pass. After, we walked in the light of the afternoon. I judged the need to evade pursuit had long since passed.

"Would you sing for me, my Warden?"

This came like a bolt out of a clear sky, and I turned to protest . . . but I knew it was useless. Had she kept anything from me? And did I not owe her so much already?

I thought back to the song she had shared with me, what felt so long ago now. My voice was awkward, and broke in places, but I sang as clear as I could manage.

Dear old Tumbledown, hear our charm.
Keep our fathers from all harm.
Keep our mothers in the light.
Let the soldiers sleep tonight.
Let the maidens pine in peace.
Grant our sickly kind release.
And us children—

It had been nearly twenty years since I had lost my brother, and yet as those final lines were about to leave my lips . . . I felt hot tears stain my cheeks, and Ailta drew me into an embrace. She knew me as her own soul, sometimes.

"Shhh," she said, as I felt the grief sting my heart as sharply as it had the night I had taken my brother's life.

The Sea

Our journey neared completion. Would I lose another dear to my heart, at its end?

I yet wore the same knife at my side.

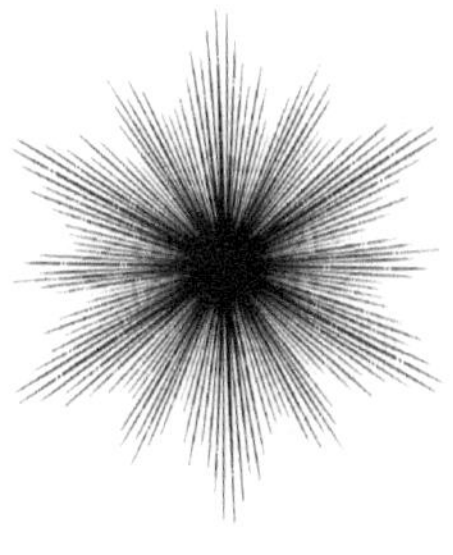

XXi.

MY TALE IS NEARLY DONE. Only a few words more.

The tomb was marked by a plain pile of sharp stones, all of them taken from the mountain screes to the north and west. It had held through the weathering of centuries, and at its base a small stone pathway led down what might have once been a simple ravine. The path jackknifed sharply against the slope, then disappeared below a tiny over-hang—hidden from the view above and blocked by a massive slab of stone.

I let Ailta take the lead. She held out the key, or whatever relic it was, and the stone parted for us.

The chill of the mountain descended on my bones as

we walked into the darkness ahead.

"Stay close," I said.

Ailta looked back, her eyes drawn and forlorn. "Of course." She knew I spoke not for her own protection, but from the yearnings of my own heart.

Yes, we had coupled—and more than once by then. Ailta was a tender lover, and I've had none since. But of our mission we had spoken little, apart from what I've told you already. Little save my plea, that night we left the Tower.

Beg leave of your Queen . . .

Ailta had said she would try, which would have to be enough. We walked down into the tomb.

It was dark. Ailta's starlight did little to dispel the gloom. The stone and dirt hung over us, forcing both of us to stoop our heads. And it was cold.

I have heard the tales of ancient tombs breached, the treasure of kings and warriors defiled. This did not feel like those tales. There was no mist picking at our ankles, no dire curse pronounced upon our hearts. Perhaps this was because we were meant to come here. The Queen, perhaps, welcomed us.

Oh, yes, I saw your Queen.

Her ossuary was not lavish. After a few minutes' descent, we came to it: a small, circular room. It was of stone, though ill kept. I saw the dance of spiderweb cracks across the walls, and was glad that our task would be done with quickly enough.

Her coffin—sarcophagus, Ailta had said—lay on a raised bier, and the stone atop it groaned open as we approached. Oh, yes, I was scared. Fear iced my veins as it would anyone come to such a scene.

A whiteness emerged from the tomb. The Queen.

Oh, I could take the easy way out. I could say that words cannot describe what there I saw. But, no. Words are poor enough, but they can do the job I set to them.

She was pearlescent, glowing with the sheen of the greater moon. She was a specter, though more solid than you might guess. Her robes flowed like mist about her, and her eyes were bright and cruel. When she spoke, the tomb quivered at her voice. It was not a voice that echoed, but stole directly into the listener's heart.

You have come, Our dutiful servants.

I realized, only then: I had no idea what, precisely, must come next.

Ailta stepped forward. "I am the lastborn of the stars, the least among those sworn to you, my Queen." She inclined her head, and the Queen put her hand atop Ailta's crown.

We accept this your devotion, lastborn of Our stars.

Then her eyes rose and fixed themselves upon mine. I stuttered, managing, "The W-warden. I . . . k-kept the way for your servant, Ailta."

The Queen did not respond in words. I inclined my head to her, and I saw her eyes acknowledge this before turning back to the star.

The life of Our body has long since departed, little star. But you will awaken it in Us.

And then the Queen placed her other hand atop Ailta's head. And I saw . . .

Starlight. It burst from Ailta, swirling around her, a smudge of celestial light. She cried out in surprise, but the Queen breathed in her radiance and smiled. Ailta's body quivered into an unnatural stillness, held in place by the

Queen's decree.

The Queen's presence . . . solidified, somewhat. And that was when I realized.

Ailta would not survive this.

My hand went directly to my knife before I hesitated, the grief I had carried for so long staying my blade. I would strike at the Queen—but she was but a spirit, one who feasted on the very essence of the star I had come to love.

I had to—

I closed my eyes, not trusting them to hide my intentions. Ailta had little time. Moments, perhaps mere seconds.

Twenty-nine years. That is what Ailta had said—the space of time she would have to wait to return, should her body perish.

Could I wait that long?

I knew then the answer waiting in the depths of my heart.

Yes, I could. Yes, I would.

I whispered, "I'm sorry," but I don't know if Ailta heard. Then I stepped forward and placed my hand upon

Ailta's shoulder. Louder, I said into her ear, "I will wait for you."

And I swear to you, I heard a response. Whether coming from her, or as the product of my desperate mind, I heard these words: "I will be there."

The knife slipped between her vertebrae like the fading whisper of twilight, as easily as it had pierced my brother twenty years ago. I saw the light leave her eyes.

And then her body died.

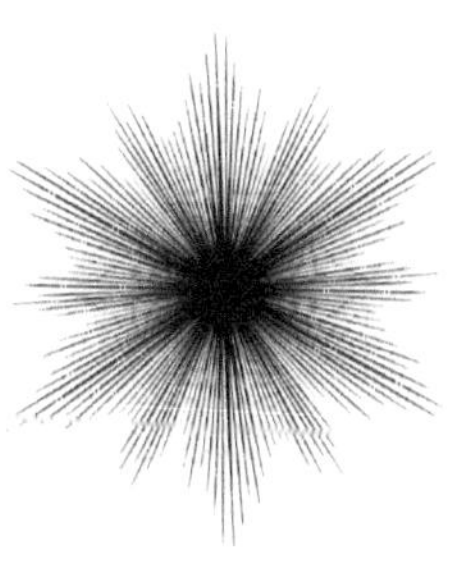

XXii.

The Queen screamed in agony, the source of Her resurrection cut off before it could even truly begin. I was thrown backward against the stone. Scrabbling, I feared for my own life, but Her anger was short lived. Her shout was cut off by a silence that echoed louder in my ears.

Darkness reigned beneath the earth. The last vestiges of starlight had flickered and died the moment I pierced Ailta's heart. I scrabbled in my pack for my tinderbox. After a few frustrating minutes, I managed a spark that caught, and I blew it into a tiny flame that fed my lantern.

Before me, Ailta's body lay still. The Queen's sarcophagus was once again sealed in stone.

I dragged Ailta's body from that place and blessed the cool mountain air that greeted my face as we emerged into the light.

Yes, I performed all the rites appropriate to inter her body. It lays there in the ground to this day.

But there was one thing I kept for myself. A bag containing a thousand shards of glass. I didn't open it there at her grave; something stopped me. But I kept it for myself.

I tore down the cairn raised above the Queen's tomb with my bare hands. It had stood for centuries—long enough already. Oh, I don't care if your Starlit Mother hears me say this. But no Queen who would steal Ailta's life from me was worthy of my worship.

The key to the tomb I left with Ailta's body. If some lucky soul should find it and open the tomb in the coming years, so be it. But I would not make it easy.

A few hours down the road, I collapsed to my knees. Adrenalin had carried me thus far—but no further. I wept; I cried my grief to the mountains, and heard only my echoes in response. Her face, her grace, her beauty and her tender love, now gone.

I would carry what I could, but I already felt so much of her slipping away from me.

My hands found the pouch of glass and I opened it, spilling those shards across my naked palm.

There was a tiny glow of starlight still trapped within that glass. And I saw that Ailta had begun her work of fixing the masterpiece, joining a few of the shards back together. It would not have looked the same had she been able to finish, but a new beauty would have been found within it.

Yes, I still have it; every shard. They have never left my side.

But the starlight. That warmed my palm, and I felt it enter into my arm, travel down to my heart. I closed my eyes and wept again.

What little starlight was left I treasured within myself. And then . . . within me, that starlight wrought a miracle, one I carried with reverence over the next nine months.

Oh, you've already guessed, yes?

Of course. That miracle, born of Ailta's light, was you.

XXiii.

IT WAS THE THIRD NIGHT when I saw Ailta in the sea above, once more. She glimmered as brightly as she had on the surface of Melodia. I stood there, far below, and swore again that I would wait for her.

My journey back to the Monastery was swift.

I will say this: the Monastery held a trial, of sorts. They would not hear the truth—it was blasphemy to any who had not seen what I had seen. Punishment was pronounced.

Not death, of course. I carried within me a miracle wrought by starlight. Anyone could see that. Anyone who looks into your shining face, child. No, for me the sentence was long imprisonment, and lashings long and cruel.

Wait. You think I gained these scars from wounds outside these walls? Oh, no. The Starlit Mother herself made a gift of them to me. But they are the least of my scars; they mar only my skin.

The Starlit Mother gave me pain, yes. It was paltry next to the wounds I'd taken in my heart. And her successor—well, she is a lesser woman. I think our newest Starlit Mother would prefer to forget me entirely.

And so I could do nothing but wait.

Oh, yes, you reckon well. I've spun this tale quite carefully, after all. This is the night—the very night when Ailta should come again to our realm. Twenty-nine years to the day have passed since I first saw her face.

Oh, I don't know. I hope, but that is the power and the weakness of hope: it holds no truth itself. I could not keep my vigil under that midnight sea down here, barred even from starlight.

Has she joined her fellow stars in death, at last?

Well, in an hour more, we both can know. You have the keeping of the keys, my child. And she is your mother, too.

I would love for you to meet her.

Oh, take your time deciding. We have a few hours yet. No matter. I am glad I have finally managed to tell you this tale. It was not easy, as you well saw. This aging mind has forgotten much more than it's remembered.

But know this, my child. Even if I do not see her like again, they will drag from me a final scream before I perish. *I still, after all this time, remember her!* Not the hundred blades of Calamity could prise that victory from my lifeless hands.

Come, child. Grant your mother a single wish. Let us walk under the sea of night and turn our eyes to the stars above.

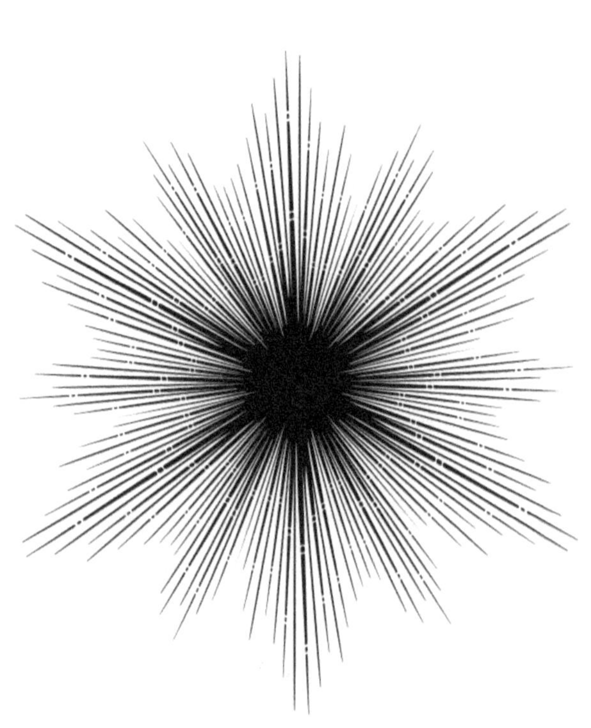

About the Author

Madeline Konrad (she / they) is the pen name of the transgender, Denver-based author of this work and (hopefully) many more sapphic fantasies to come. She enjoys long walks in the mountains, a good plate of sushi, and scrolling through queer tumblr until the posts start to repeat.

Speaking of which, one might possibly summon her at: madi-konrad.tumblr.com, toot.lgbt/@madikonrad, @madikonrad.bsky.social, or by gazing up at a clear, summer sky after sunset while composing a sonnet with clear sapphic subtext.

She may also be emailed at madeline.konrad@proton.me (good vibes only!)

About Pink Hydra Press

Founded in 2024 to make a space for new, queer, and weird speculative literature, Pink Hydra Press is the only organization of its kind in Africa. The genre/lit magazine The Pink Hydra has published short stories and poems from dozens of international authors. The book press is just starting out.

If you enjoy stories with a touch of the weird, or if you're an author who loves writing books and poetry infused with weirdness, come visit us at www.thepinkhydra.com.

We publish a variety of genres, but we are particularly interested in queer science fiction and fantasy, stories written by and about women, stories which challenge the current status quo, and spicy romantic and erotic stories.

Many heads. One mission.

MJÖLNIR,
GUNGNIR &
GJALLARHORN
Six heroic tales from the Norse mythology
Retold by
Matias Travieso-Diaz
. . . a must-read for fans of Norse mythology and short stories!
— As reviewed on Amazon.com

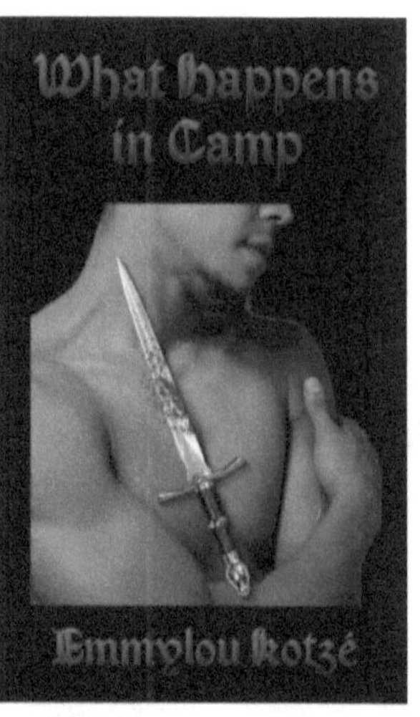

What Happens
in Camp
Emmylou Kotzé

FOREST OF THE
MORNING
EMMYLOU KOTZÉ

"Maarten and Johanna are characters you will
take into your heart and treasure."
—ERIC KAPLAN, writer and producer,
THE BIG BANG THEORY
HELEN
DE CRUZ
THE ARTISTRY
OF MAGIC

Visit our online stores:

ko-fi.com/thepinkhydra/shop

thepinkhydra.itch.io

. . . or anywhere else where (e)books are sold.